The Secret
★ of the ★
Water Knight

Also by Rusalka Reh:

Pizzicato: The Abduction of the Magic Violin
This Brave Balance

The Secret ★ of the ★ Water Knight

Rusalka ★ Reh

TRANSLATED BY ★ Katy Derbyshire

Illustrations by Eva Schöffmann-Davidov

PUBLISHED BY

amazon crossing ◉

Text copyright © 2008 Verlag Friedrich Oetinger GmbH
English translation copyright © 2011 by Amazon Content Services LLC
Illustrations © 2008 Eva Schöffmann-Davidov
All rights reserved.
Printed in the United States of America

The Secret of Water Knight by Rusalka Reh was first published in 2008 by Verlag Friedrich Oetinger as *Das Geheimnis des Wasserritters*.
Translated from German by Katy Derbyshire.
First published in the U.S. in 2011 by AmazonCrossing.

Published by AmazonCrossing
P.O. Box 400818
Las Vegas, NV 89140

ISBN-13: 9781611090062
ISBN-10: 1611090067
Library of Congress Control Number: 2010918616

For Anna Katharina

Stillness—

the cicada's cry

drills into the rocks.

Matsuo Bash ō
(Japanese poet, translated by Robert Hass)

Contents

⋆1⋆
Swimming

"Jump!" shouted Leon.

"She's too chicken," said Yolanda.

"Come on, Kat, just jump!" called Isabel.

"She's such a wuss." Marek laughed.

"Shall I give her a push?" asked Jan.

"Hey, look what she's doing now!" David snickered and pointed.

At me.

I'm Kat.

I was standing on the one-meter board, standing right at the very edge. But I didn't have the guts to jump—it was dumb, I know, and chicken, but I didn't have the guts, even though I'm ten years old. All around me, the other kids were screaming with glee, their voices bouncing off the smooth, blue tiled walls like in a bad dream. If only it had been a bad dream! But this was real. Unfortunately.

Instead of leaping in like all the others, I sat down on the front of the board, dangled my legs like two wet sacks, and started to cry. And then the pool attendant came over, just to make everything worse.

"What's up with the kid?" she asked, her hands on her hips.

Ms. Eckhart, our teacher, shrugged her shoulders—she didn't know what was up with me. I didn't even really know myself. All I knew was that I was scared.

The other kids in my class were standing behind me. Leon was hopping from one leg onto the other, and Yolanda was rubbing her arms. I couldn't jump—no, there was no way I'd dare. So I stood up again, swayed back along the diving board, and climbed down the ladder. Everyone looked at me like a nasty stain on their favorite T-shirt. It's not nice being looked at like that.

"Kat?" Mom asked when I was in bed that evening. She was tucking the covers in around me a little longer than usual. "What do you think about a vacation by the sea?"

"Why?" I asked, suspicious already. "Why by the sea?"

Mom sat down next to me.

"I heard you're really scared of swimming lessons, and I thought we could practice a little on vacation on an island." She stroked my cheek. "Just a little—no pressure," she added quickly.

"Did Ms. Eckhart tell you that?" I asked, my ears burning. What a tattletale.

"Yes, she called today." Mom cleared her throat. "So what do you say? Summer vacation starts soon."

What a tattletale, old Eckhart, I thought again, and I pulled the cover up to my chin. I was ashamed to be the only kid in my class who still couldn't swim. But actually it wasn't swimming I was really afraid of. Not exactly, anyway. I just hated it when my head went underwater. I even held a washcloth in front of my eyes when I washed my hair, and when I got water in my ears—oh no, that was just awful!

Well, anyway, I always stretched my head out of the pool like a giraffe at swim practice, and then the thing with my arms and legs kind of didn't work. And apart from that, a giraffe neck like that looks pretty dumb. All I needed was a rubber bathing cap with flowers on it—then I'd be the perfect old lady!

I wiggled my toes a little under the covers, tucked in nice and tight now.

I've never been to the ocean, I thought. It must be nice there. After a little while I asked, "And what if I don't learn to swim? Will you guys still love me?"

Just to be on the safe side.

"Grandma can't swim either, sweetheart," answered Mom, patting my bedcover as though it were a horse's backside.

She often answers my questions like that, so that I have to think of my own right answer. We all love Grandma a lot, I thought, I mean a whole lot, with hugging and kissing and gifts and all that. And it's never made a difference that she can't swim.

"All right then," I said, and I snuggled further down in my warm, dry bed.

"It's a deal," said Mom with a smile, and then she stood up and flicked out the light.

So on the first Monday of summer vacation, we took a flight in the dead of night and landed on an island in the early morning, just as the sun was coming up pale yellow behind the hills on the horizon, bathing everything around us in honeyed light.

Ten minutes ago, we arrived with our suitcases and bags at a very pretty house with thick stone walls and a tall palm tree growing next to it.

And that's right where I am now.

Mom, Dad, and I climb a narrow staircase. The walls are painted a dark shade of pink with a green patterned border printed along them.

"What a pretty frieze!" says Mom, gasping and gazing at the walls in awe, as though we were in a church and not a guesthouse.

Dad just wheezes away quietly. He has to carry a huge backpack and two suitcases—he doesn't care either way about the "frieze." On the third floor, Mom looks first at the key rings with our room numbers on them, and then at the few doors along the corridor lined with thick red carpet.

"Here's your room," she says, pointing to a white wooden door with the number nine on it.

She hands me a brass key. Then she drops her suitcase onto its wheels and pulls it along behind Dad.

Outside the next door, Dad says, "And this is our room, right next to yours."

He puts the key in the lock.

"We'll come get you in a minute, OK?"

I nod and unlock my door.

My room is beautiful.

It has a gray stone floor with blue stars on it. On the right is a wooden bed with flowers carved into it, and on the left is a white-painted closet. Next to the window is a dressing table with a mirror and a stool, which I guess I won't need because I don't have any makeup or perfume to put on. But it still looks good, like in an old movie!

I throw my suitcase on the bed, open the window as wide as it can go, and lean out. I close my eyes, holding my face out in the air, and all of a sudden there's a gurgling tickle in my belly! There are birds chirping like crazy, and it smells so good you wouldn't believe it. It makes me think of oranges and a little bit of lavender. I open my eyes again because it's funny looking out of a window with your eyes shut.

And then I see something very odd—there's a rope ladder dangling from my windowsill! It reaches down almost to the ground, and it sways to and fro when I touch it. Just as I'm starting to wonder why there's a ladder hanging from my window and who used it before me—or if it's been put there especially for me, and if so, why—there's a knock at my door.

It's Dad in a terribly good mood. He pinches my cheek and beams at me.

"So, let's make a brisky-brisk start, huh? We'll look for a quiet corner for you to practice your swimming in peace!"

Dad often uses funny words like "brisky-brisk," which nobody except him ever uses because he thinks them up himself. What he means is "brisk," of course. Actually, "brisk" is funny enough already, as a word, I mean. But never mind. Outfitted with huge beach towels, factor-30 sun lotion, water bottles in a yellow beach bag, and straw sun hats on our heads, we set out ten minutes later—Mom, Dad, and me.

It's boiling hot, and everything in the distance is all unfocused and flickery, like in a movie about the desert. The crickets are buzzing up a racket.

"Crickets are called cicadas here," says Mom. And then she warbles, "Isn't it just wonderful here?" stroking a white flower in a concrete plant pot in passing, as though it were a Siamese kitten. She makes a face like she's been washed in fabric conditioner.

All right then, cicadas, I think. That gurgly happiness from before is as though blown away. We're not here to have fun! I'm supposed to be learning something!

I dawdle along, pretending I'm looking at everything very closely, but really I'm just playing for time because

I feel sick with fear every time I think about learning to swim. The sun's shining yellow and white, the sky's shining bright blue, the flowers are shining purple, red, and orange, beach umbrellas are shining green and white, pumped-up airbeds people carry around like briefcases jammed under people's arms are shining in all sorts of colors.

We walk along through all this shining, and I keep thinking, "Learning to swim is brisky-brisk dumb; learning to swim is brisky-brisk dumb," as though an old record had got stuck in a groove in my mind.

All of a sudden, the air smells to me of moldy oranges, and that puts me in a really bad mood. I stare silently at the sidewalk as I walk along, hiding deep inside myself. I almost feel like I'm falling asleep. But I keep on walking. I walk and walk and…

Suddenly we're standing on a narrow path.

There's no one in sight. All the people have vanished. I look around, surprised.

On my left, pine trees rise sharply toward the sky, and I lean my head all the way back to catch sight of their tips. On the right is a low stone wall, and behind it I finally spot the dark blue sea. It looks so gorgeous! White crowns of foam are dancing on the waves. There's a smell of salt and fishes. And of the needles on the trees. A gull screeches above the water, held in place by the wind.

"How funny—there's not a soul here but us," says Dad, looking around as though he expected other families to leap out from behind the trees at any moment. But that doesn't happen. There's just nobody here but us.

"Look, there's a little door in the wall over there!"

Mom walks over to a barred gate and tries out the rusty handle. The gate swings open, slamming against the wall with a clatter. Curious, Dad and I step up to Mom's side. We see a staircase leading down along a steep cliff. At the bottom is a square bathing spot made of smooth gray stone. Around the beach, the water is dark blue and very deep.

"This is definitely the right spot for your swimmy-swim lessons!" Dad grins and pats my shoulder.

Swimmy-swim lessons. Oh dear. I take a deep breath, walk through the little entrance, close the gate, and traipse down the stairs behind Mom and Dad.

Even though I'm supposed to learn to swim here, I really like the place right away. The wind suddenly lifts my braids right up, as though they were two scraps of paper, and then it lays them gently back on my shoulders. The light shimmers like when you look through soap bubbles. And the quiet. I listen as closely as I can. But it's really and truly quiet here.

Slowly, I take off my clothes, sit down on my new towel in my new bathing suit, and stare at the sea. The deep, dark blue water is the only thing wrong with this beautiful place, if you ask me.

Dad picks up a pebble lying lonely on the concrete floor.

"Hey look, it looks like a peppermint with a pale green pattern," he says, holding it up in front of my face.

Then he leans slightly to one side and launches the pebble from the hip, like a cowboy drawing his Colt and shooting. The stone bounces once, twice, three times, four times off the calm seawater before it sinks.

"Seven times!" Dad calls out, patting his hands clean on his swim trunks.

Dad's sometimes not too good at counting either.

"So, Eva honey, shall we go for a dip?"

He winks over at Mom, gesturing at the water with his chin. Mom skips like a gazelle, obviously very pleased and excited. How can she?

"Don't they have a shallow end around here?" I complain quietly, but no one hears me, and I know perfectly well there isn't one. This is the ocean, the briny sea, and it doesn't care a smidge about poor little kids who can't swim.

Mom and Dad dive headfirst into the water, and I hardly hear a splash at all, they're so elegant about it. I'll never be able to do that like them, that's for sure, I think. I'm almost mad that they can do something so incredibly well and I can't do it at all. Panting and laughing, they wave over at me.

"The water's just great!" Papa yells over at me. "We'll start your practice in an hour or so, OK, then you can play first." He gives me the world's happiest wave and calls out, "Playerini, playerinski!"

"Whatever," I answer feebly.

Dad's one of a kind, I swear.

A few minutes later the two of them come back soaking wet, giggling and kissing each other, and lie down on their stomachs with their heads on the big beach towels. I prop myself up on my elbows. The sea's making a beautiful sound, and the air's hot. I get very sleepy. A huge mosquito lands on my lower arm. I blow at it, and it tries to cling onto the hairs on my arm like tree trunks in a stormy forest. In the end it gives up and flies away. It hasn't stung me. Mom and Dad's breathing is calm and even. They've fallen asleep!

And then it's as though I hear someone calling my name, from a long way away, but so clearly that I can understand it perfectly well. Maybe I've got sunstroke, I think, and I put on my straw hat.

"Kat," I hear again, quietly but urgently, from a long way off. "Ka-at." It sounds like murmuring, rustling, like something that's been there a long time, so you forget to even hear it.

Strange. Nobody knows me here, and I don't know anybody either. And we're here alone. When I squint toward the light, I spot a little outcrop of rock nearby. I get up. All of a sudden, I just have to know what's hiding behind that rock.

★2★
Breathing

Big waves wash over the concrete floor, and the seaweed spread across it like wet green hair is pretty slippery. I straddle it with a leap and land with my bare feet on a narrow, dry concrete walkway. It leads right around the corner that just got me so curious.

I take a cautious look around the rock. Nothing out of the ordinary, I think with relief. The little path takes another bend to the left a few yards on, leading further along the cliff. After that it comes to a sudden end. And then all there is is the deep blue sea.

Step by step, I walk along the concrete path, which burns very hot under the soles of my feet. It's kind of scary here, but I don't know why. I can't see Mom and Dad from here.

I listen very closely. To begin with, all I can hear is the splashing of the waves like a quiet, never-changing song.

It laps closer and ebbs away, laps closer, ebbs away again, laps closer, ebbs…

But then there's something else.

What's that sound? It's not someone calling like a moment ago, that's for sure. It's coming from further back, from the cliff, almost at the end of the narrow path.

Even though the sound is very, very creepy, I keep walking slowly, feeling the hot concrete under my feet and hearing the splashing. And the sound gets clearer and clearer. In the end it's right up close to me.

I step up to the cliff and spot a hole in a jutting stone surface, about the size of a car tire. Very carefully, I peep over the edge of the hole. It leads straight downward, as black as pitch and as dark as night, in the middle of the warm, sandy yellow rock. And there! There it is again!

I hold my breath in shock because what I hear there is nothing other than *breathing*. Someone or something is breathing. In and out, in and out.

My heart starts thumping wildly. I look up and get another shock right there: a fat yellow toad is perched on the rock above me. It's as big as a soccer ball. The toad's green eyes are staring at me, right at me: *Kat*.

I turn on my heel as fast as I can, first running around one corner and then sliding around the next, straddling the spot with the slippery seaweed and making so much noise that Mom and Dad both raise their heads at the same time. When I come to a halt in front of them, they look at me as though they didn't know who I am. They both have red marks and stripes on their cheeks, pressed in by their towels. It looks very strange.

"You wanted to teach me to swim!" I call out much too loudly, breathing heavily from the huge shock and the running.

Dad doesn't notice how upset I am, but he's still amazed. At last his daughter wants to learn to swim, he thinks. He leaps to his feet with joy.

"Then hop right into the water, my little froggy!" he says—not noticing me flinching at the last word.

A metal ladder leads directly down to the sea from the bathing terrace. I cling onto it tightly. The water's scarily cold, and it climbs up me as I inch down the ladder, as though it were fear itself.

"Come on," Dad says in a kind voice, holding his arms out to me. "You can hold onto me to start with, and I'll tell you what you need to know. Now listen carefully..."

I listen mighty carefully and clutch onto Dad, but the whole swimming thing's just really scary. How am I supposed to stay on top of the water? I'm a whole human being, and I'm far too heavy!

Now Dad's holding onto me under my belly.

"I'm gonna let go!" he calls out. "And you try on your own, OK? And don't stick your neck out like a giraffe!"

The minute he takes his hand away, I start kicking like a cat someone's thrown into a canal.

"Frog kicks!" Dad shouts over at me.

I've forgotten everything he just told me—move your arms and legs like a frog, keep your head low, all that.

I wave wildly with everything I can move, but I still go under, swallowing a huge mouthful of saltwater. I come up again, coughing and sinking straight underwater again. And again! At last, Dad has mercy and catches hold of me. I throw my arms around his neck and clutch hold of him. I cough and cough and cough.

"I want to get out," I sob, feeling hot drips of water running out of my eyes and down my face, cold as seawater.

"Shhh, shhh," says Dad.

He climbs up the ladder with me and lays me so carefully on my towel as though I were sick, and that's how I feel too.

"Shhh," he says again, sitting down next to me.

I look at the sea as if it were Mr. Kegler, our mean old math teacher.

"Hold on," says Mom. "I've got something here to help you get your strength back."

She reaches for a cardboard box printed with "Belgian Butter Cookies," pulls out the plastic packaging, and frowns.

"It's empty," she says. "Andrew?" She turns to Dad. "Don't tell me you've eaten all the cookies!"

Dad tilts his head and raises his eyebrows.

"Do I look like Cookie Monster, Eva?"

He opens his eyes wide and growls, "COOOOK-IIIIIEEES!"

Mom raises her eyes heavenward, shaking the pack and then her head.

"But it was a brand new pack! Kat, did you maybe…?"

"Do *I* look like Cookie Monster?" I ask, coughing a little so she knows I have other problems than Belgian butter cookies right now.

"Strange," murmurs Mom, "I don't know what's happened to them, but never mind."

She puts the pack back in her yellow beach bag.

"You know what?" she says then with a smile at me. "We'll forget the swimming for today. I'll show you something much better."

She reaches into her bag again and pulls out a huge pair of goggles with a built-in rubber nose and a tube at one side.

"You don't have to be able to swim to go snorkeling," she explains, putting on the goggles. "It's really fun—you just lie on top of the water and float automatically. Only your face goes underwater."

Mom adjusts the rubber nose and pokes the end of the tube in her mouth. She looks at me through the glass like an owl. I can't help laughing. She peels the goggles off her face again and hands them to me.

"You put them on!"

So I pull on the goggles and a pair of water wings. Yes, water wings! So what? No one can see me here, can they? Then I walk back over to the metal ladder. Mom stands right behind me, watching. Carefully, I climb down the rungs. Once again, the cold water creeps up my body. I don't like it one bit, but at least I'm used to it now. And once I'm finally standing up to my neck in the water and lay my face in the goggles on top of it, I'm absolutely captivated! I forget the world up there. Belgian cookies, towels, the sun, Mom and Dad—all of them disappear at that moment, as though I'd fallen asleep.

A huge school of glittering blue fish is suspended in the water in front of my eyes, above each other, below each other, and alongside each other. They all look in my direction, not moving. Seaweed snakes pale green across the ground, and I almost believe it's a forest where the fish are out on a Sunday stroll. Close to my legs, a fish with a reddish-orange dress of scales nibbles along the rock face. Slightly further away, a crab vanishes sharply into a gap between two stones. And it's quiet down here, absolutely quiet. All I can hear is my own breathing, like rustling from a distant, secret time.

I keep my face on top of the water and push off from the ladder. I don't think of my fear of getting my head underwater for one moment. I want to move over to the tiny fish that look like they're hanging from a mobile. Gently, I paddle my feet and come gradually closer to the fish. Once I get right near them, they shoot away to the left and right like arrows, making way for me. It's like a dance or fireworks, only silent, absolutely silent.

I keep paddling forward where the fish have made way for me. Then I look down. Something's moving there, detaching itself from the ground as though in slow motion. It's a fish, as flat as a Frisbee, and it starts to flutter like a bird. Sand billows up to me in clouds. Gracefully, the fish rises upward through the clouds of sand. It comes closer and closer, seeming to get larger and larger. I'm just about to navigate away so I'm not blocking its path, when something very strange happens.

A jerk passes through its body, and at that very same moment I spot something flying slowly through the water. I reach out my hands to catch it.

"Come back tonight, and use this whistle!" the Frisbee gasps. Its eyes dart restlessly in every direction. "We from the Lunalos bathing terrace wish you the very best of luck for your mission! I have to go now—the vile toad mustn't notice we've been talking. And don't forget—come back tonight! *Adiós!*"

The fish gradually sinks back down to where it came from.

I call after it, "But...who is the vile...what mission?" But now it's disappeared into thin air, or thin water if you like. It's certainly vanished without a trace. I stare at what I'm holding in my hands. It's a whistle made of mother-of-pearl, shimmering white and pink. I'm just about to put it in my mouth in place of my snorkel when something grabs me by the shoulders! Out of shock, I spit out the snorkel and swallow water. Oh no, what is it?

"Kat!" I hear a voice. And again, "Kat!"

Is it the vile toad? Or some giant fish? A sea monster? A conger eel? A...

I struggle to the surface, gasping for air.

And there's Mom, right next to me.

"Kat, my goodness!" She's swimming breaststroke on the spot, her eyes so wide that she really looks a bit like a monster. "Come out of the water right now—you're all blue in the face!"

I quickly grab hold of Mom's back—I've instantly remembered I can't really swim, only snorkel, and that's how we make it back to the bathing terrace a few moments later.

Dad curses like a sailor.

"First you're so scared you wet your pants and can't swim a stroke, and then you disappear! Do you know how far away you were?" he asks, looking at me angrily. His face is pale.

"No," I answer sheepishly, looking at my fingertips, which are rather blue. My ears are still burning though.

"Mom found you behind that corner over there!" Dad waves his hand vaguely. "She swam out to look for you because we couldn't see you anywhere from here." He takes my arm tightly and shakes me. "Just think if you'd drowned!"

Mom and Dad keep telling me off until it starts to get dark, and then they stuff everything in the yellow beach bag, still describing all the terrible things that might have happened to me if Mom hadn't rescued me at the last moment. I don't say anything, even though I hate it when they're mad at me.

Right in the middle of the telling off and lecturing, Dad suddenly curses. "For heaven's sake!" he says, his hands raised to his head.

Something clatters on the concrete.

"What's up? What's the matter?" asks Mom, concerned.

Dad bends down to pick something up.

"It looks like…" he murmurs. "No, it can't be."

He's holding a pebble. White, with a green pattern. The stone looks like—a peppermint. It's shiny with water.

Annoyed, Dad drops the peppermint pebble again, and it rolls across the concrete into the dusk with a bright, cheerful clatter. He shoves Mom and me toward the stairs, puffing and panting. Up at the top, he shuts the gate behind us determinedly.

I take a last look around.

Everything is submerged in blue light. The waves swish quietly against the wall.

A pair of green eyes looks up at me from the terrace.

At me, Kat.

It's the fat yellow toad.

With one clawed paw, it's stuffing oval yellow circles into its mouth.

Our Belgian butter cookies.

I'm not kidding.

★3★
Whistle

The moon shines brightly through my window. I can see all the things in my room. My ears are pricked up just like when my next-door neighbor's cat Selma listens out for a mouse in the grass. After about half an hour, I can tell Mom and Dad have fallen asleep in the next room.

As quiet as a mouse, I slip out of bed, put on my jeans, T-shirt, and sneakers, and creep over to the window. I turn the strange whistle over in my hands in the moonlight, and then I put it in my pocket. What did the Frisbee fish mean when it talked about my "mission" and the "vile toad"? What does it all mean?

The window casements are wide apart like an open book, and a warm lavender wind blows across my face from outside. I swing my legs up onto the windowsill and climb down the rope ladder. I have to take a jump from the bottom rung. There's a loud crunching sound as my feet land on the gravel, and a dog starts barking in the next garden.

"Quiet down," I whisper. "That's a good dog. Be quiet." Ducking down, I run all the way around the house to the front entrance, and then out on the street.

The narrow roads in the village are empty. I walk very fast. It's warm, and the wind strokes around me like a begging kitten. Soon there are fewer houses and fewer streetlamps. Now I have to rely on the moonlight. The moon is clear and large, with just a tiny sliver missing until it's full. Around it is an orange crown, like the halo around Baby Jesus's head in churches.

I'm so glad the moon's shining so brightly!

Silent, I look at the ground as I walk, hiding deep inside myself. It's almost as though I were falling asleep. But I keep walking on.

I walk and walk, and at that very moment I notice I'm back on the narrow coastal path again. I spot the wall on my right; on the left, the tall pine trees rise up into the dark sky. The gate is right in front of my nose. I turn its rusty handle, and it swings open with a squeak. I step inside.

I've hardly closed the gate behind me when I get that strange feeling again. It's so quiet. I climb down the steps. The sea lies calm before me, glittering. I cross the bathing terrace and look out to sea from the edge.

I blow into the whistle with all my might, screwing up my face in anticipation of a loud sound. But no sound comes out. I blow again. Nothing.

What's wrong with this strange whistle? "Oh no!" I say quietly, shaking it. "Aren't you working?"

I try again. The sea remains quiet. Nothing moves on the bathing terrace either.

Suddenly, I see a silvery back emerging from the water, and then I hear a very low voice.

"At last! You're here at last!"

It's a dolphin, stretching his beak out of the waves and looking at me! But how timid he sounds. I always thought dolphins were happy, leaping and laughing and sharing their joy. What on earth's the matter with this one?

He swims closer to me. A wave slaps against the terrace wall, and I smell the ocean.

"Welcome to Lunalos, our bathing terrace, noble Kat! I am the Water Knight."

I've never heard such a deeply sad voice before, even though it's saying such friendly things.

"I don't understand at all!" I say. "What do you all want from me?"

The dolphin says quietly, "You can free Lunalos at last, at long last."

He's lying in the water, looking terribly weak. I'm almost worried he might be slammed against the terrace wall by the next wave and hurt himself.

He continues in a dark voice. "For four hundred and ninety-nine full moons, we have been trapped under her curse."

"Under *her* curse?" I ask impatiently. "What do you mean?"

He gives me an earnest look and says, "The old ones tell us young ones of a toad. An ugly, yellow toad. She lives in an underwater cavern, not far from here."

He points his beak in the direction of where I saw the breathing hole and the yellow toad that afternoon.

"She takes parts of human bodies away and leaves them something fishy in their place," he continues, and I realize I'm scared of the toad even now, when he's just telling me about it. Something fishy? What does he mean by that? But he's still talking.

"Hardly anyone has ever caught sight of her. But most know her from bad dreams. Since she's been in power, there have been awful storms that destroy everything over and over again! All this is a terrible nightmare for us. We call her the 'vile toad.'"

"But why does she do all that?" I interrupt the Water Knight.

He falls silent for a moment.

"Her soul is dark," he whispers after a while. Nothing more. Now he swims to and fro, the moonlight glinting on his back. It's as though something in his slim, weak body were coming to life.

"And at the five hundredth full moon, the moonlight will fall with special strength on the underwater entrance to the cavern, which is otherwise blocked off by a stone. The cave opens for this one night, but then it closes again at sunrise and stays closed for the next five hundred full moons. Only in this one night can anyone enter."

Luckily, I'm pretty "brisky-brisk" at mental arithmetic, so I work it out as quick as a flash: five hundred full moons equals five hundred months, divided by twelve because a year has twelve months, which equals about forty years. Wow. That's a long time!

It looks almost as though the Water Knight were just about to take an elegant jump. But instead, he carries on telling me the story in an agitated tone. "When the vile toad is conquered, all her enchantments will come undone! Our fear will vanish! Lunalos and the entire island will be beautiful again! And I…" he hesitates, "I will be able to jump again! For so many years, I have been lame with fear of the vile toad."

So that's why he seems so sad and weak, I think.

All of a sudden, I feel excited and confused.

"But why m-me? Why should I be the one to free L-Lunalos?" I stutter.

The Water Knight hesitates again for a moment.

"It has to be a human being who confronts her. And it has to be a girl. That's what the old ones tell us. And you sought us out here yesterday, just in time to help us plan our rescue," he says, looking surprised.

At that moment, I remember the breathing hole. Was it the Water Knight I'd heard breathing?

A sudden wind rustles the pine trees above our heads.

"What do I have to do?" I ask, crossing my arms across my chest. I don't feel at all comfortable about any of it.

"On the night of the full moon, you must dive down, enter the vile toad's cave, and wipe her out at last," explains the Water Knight. His words sound much brighter than a moment before. "If you summon me beforehand on the whistle, I will accompany you to the entrance and stand guard outside."

I'm so shocked I can't get a word out. My arms slide down my body and hang limply by my sides, as though they didn't belong to me anymore. I'm supposed to swim? And dive underwater on top of that? Doesn't anyone here know I can't do that? As I'm thinking all this, the Water

Knight goes on talking, but what he says seems far away. As though through cotton wool, I hear his words.

"The whistle will help you. You have to blow on it and look the toad directly in the eyes with all your might. She can't stand up to both together. That's what the old ones of Lunalos tell us. Only in this full moon night can she be attacked."

I stare at the black sea for a while. The moonlight is now only painting a slim, silvery strip on it. I see that a few clouds have gathered. It can't be true, I think. I must be dreaming. Maybe I'll wake up in a minute. I wait a while—but I don't wake up.

"I can't do it," I say at last. My tongue feels heavy. "I can't help you."

The Water Knight stares at me in shock. I gaze at my sneakers. The wind is rustling louder and louder now, and pine needles fall at my feet.

"But why not?" he asks after a pause.

His voice is instantly grayer and duller; I can hear the difference clearly. All of a sudden I'm cold. I pinch my arms to warm up—and perhaps in case it might wake me up after all.

"Because I can't swim properly, and least of all under-water," is my insolent answer.

I'm really mad.

I turn on my heel. I have to get out of here! What does all this stuff have to do with me? Nothing! I can feel the Water Knight watching me leave, his eyes weighing me down like a schoolbag on my back with at least twenty books in it. On the steps, I turn around again.

"Perhaps you'll find someone else who can save Lunalos," I say, but I can tell my voice sounds very small and weak.

As he swims away, I hear the Water Knight say, "No, *you* are the one who can save Lunalos, for you heard us at the right time."

His words echo terribly in my ears.

The Water Knight continues: "I will give everyone the news that you don't want to help, and that there's no hope of rescue."

He dives down to the depths.

"I do *want* to, I just *can't!*" I shout, angry.

But he's gone.

And then I get a bad feeling.

I look up at the sky. More and more clouds are gathering, coming together in a lump above my head. I hear a sudden roll of thunder in the distance, pushing ahead like a steam engine. And then it starts to rain. Lightning flashes in the sky, blinding me with a light so bright that it hurts my eyes. The sea, so calm before, is now raging. I look over to the horizon and see a huge wave rolling towards Lunalos from the distance.

I cower down quickly, balling myself up. I can feel the thunderclaps deep in my chest. Thunder and lightning are coming at the same time now. With a frightening creak and crash, a branch breaks off a tree and plunges onto the terrace, right next to me. Then one falls on my back! I feel as though I were being beaten up. I fold my hands above my head, screw up my eyes, and duck down even lower. Pinecones as large as men's fists roll across the ground, coming to a stop around me. Now the first huge wave crashes against the Lunalos wall, the white foam creeping up to my shoes within seconds. I hear some kind of rumble, roll to one side as fast as I can, and in the next moment a large stone from the wall above is hurled to the ground next to me.

My heart racing, I jump up. Water squelches in my sneakers, and my braids are heavy and stiff with rain. I run to the staircase, take two steps at once, wrench open the gate, and slam it behind me.

I have to get out of here! As fast as I can!

But instead of running, I suddenly freeze as though I'd forgotten something.

My whole body is trembling.

Slowly, I turn around.

And on the steps, just behind the gate, squats the big yellow toad, staring at me.

★4★

The Newspaper Man

"They say there was a pretty bad storm last night."
Mom takes a bite of her breakfast roll. The sun's
shining on the back of her head, making her pale blonde
hair glow like an angel's. For a tiny moment, I think about
whether to tell her about the vile toad, the Water Knight,
the whistle, about everything. But then I decide it's got
nothing to do with Mom and Dad. It's my business.

"They said on the radio that the people from the weather
station were taken by surprise—there was no sign that such
a bad storm was on its way." Mom frowns and takes a sip
of coffee. "There were even broken windows and demol-
ished roofs from falling branches in the early hours of the
morning," she says. "I didn't hear a thing." She looks over
at Dad. "Did you?"

"I slept like a buried dog's bone," says Dad, shaking his
head. He taps at his egg with a spoon.

"Did you notice anything, Kat?" he asks me. "You know—thunderola, lighty-lightning?"

Oh, Dad!

"Me? No, nothing," I lie, taking a quick sip of my orange juice. "I didn't notice anything."

My ears are burning again. Thank goodness my braids cover them up. I silently hope that my wet shoes and the clothes I had on at Lunalos last night will soon dry out in the sun on my windowsill.

"You've got something in your hair," says Mom, picking something out. "A little piece of bark and a pine needle," she says, holding them out in front of me. She gives me a playful nudge. "You're turning into a real little nature lover here, aren't you?"

I choke on my juice, coughing and wheezing.

"Mmm," I murmur as my eyes water, and Mom pats me on the back.

"Katinka," she says, and she only ever calls me Katinka when she means really well, "Dad and I've decided to hold your swimming lessons on the shallow sandy beach here in the village so you're not as scared as yesterday. What do you think?"

I honestly don't know what to think. Because deep down, I'm really ashamed to be such a coward, with not a drop of courage.

"All right," I mumble into my glass.

Something's feeling uncomfortable in my pocket. I reach into it and extract the whistle.

"Oh, isn't that lovely! Let me have a look!" Dad reaches out a hand.

I stuff the whistle hastily back into my pocket.

"You're not allowed to see it," I rush out. "It's…it's for your birthday!"

My heart is galloping.

"Oh, my little scampy-amp!" says Dad, stroking my head.

I knew it all along—the shallow water on the fine sand beach doesn't make learning to swim any easier at all. The only difference is the whole crowd of other children giggling and watching while Dad shouts, "Frog kicks!" for the hundredth time, and I swallow water and flounder about like crazy. Luckily, we don't practice for very long, and then Mom and Dad want to go shopping in the village.

"Our little frog's doing quite well, Eva," Dad says to Mom, putting an arm around her shoulder.

"Hey, what did we say?" Mom says and ruffles my hair.

It feels to me like I can't swim at all.

We walk along the narrow streets. They seemed so different last night, full of secrets and whisperings. Now there's barely space between all the people ambling along the sidewalks. They're all wearing shorts or skirts. Some of them are even walking around in bikinis or bathing trunks! It's gotten so hot again that everyone's constantly slurping ice cream or drinking something. Dogs are lying rolled up in shady corners, their tongues lolling out.

There are things dangling from the rooftops of all the stores: straw bags, dolls, inflatable beach balls, colorful swim rings, nets holding buckets and shovels and sand toys, flip-flops. Actually, I've wanted a set of colorful plastic bocce balls for playing with on the beach for a long time, and normally I'd beg and plead with Mom and Dad until they gave in and got me one.

But today I don't care, for some reason. It's as though I have a helmet on my head, which makes everything seem far away: the voices, the cars, the droning and ringing and buzzing of all the arcade games the older kids are playing on, and their screams when they win. I'm thinking of Lunalos. There's a smell of sun lotion on the air. The asphalt's hot, the air's hot, my clothes are sticking to my skin, and the huge sun is suspended in the sky, blinding me.

"Can you go and get us a newspaper, honey?" Dad hands me a couple of coins. "Mom and I'll just be in the shoe store over there." He points at the place. "I need a new pair of sandals. You don't want to come with us, do you, my little froggy?"

I shake my head and take the money.

"You like the newspaper man, don't you? You talked to him so long when we arrived yesterday. We'll come and pick you up in a moment," says Mom.

The two of them stroll off hand in hand.

I head for the newspaper stand. I've never seen so many newspapers and magazines in one place back home! The little hut is covered in newspapers like candy on the witch's house from "Hansel and Gretel." The newspaper man peeps out of a little window. He smiles at me. I really do like him.

"*Hola, Señorita* Kat," he says. "*Cómo estás?*"

That's Spanish—it means, "Hello, Miss Kat. How are you?"

"Fine, *gracias, señor* newspaper man," I answer, but I'm not looking at him. I'm looking at today's paper; there are at least ten copies hanging from the board above his head. The newspaper is especially for tourists, and that's why I can read what it says:

"New Thunderstorm Disaster!
Major Damages!
Meteorologists Failed Again?"

I get an uneasy feeling when I think of last night's storm and the toad. Behind my thoughts, I hear the newspaper man talking.

"So did your dad buy you the bocce balls? Did you go to Pedro's restaurant last night? You've already got a tan!"

As he chats away happily, I turn around and spot Mom and Dad a few doors behind me. They walk into the shoe store. I turn back again, reach into my pocket, and pull out a couple of coins.

"*Por favor,*" I say to the newspaper man, smiling and pointing at the paper. I put the coins on the little saucer between us.

"Here we are, *Señorita* Kat, one copy of *El día de la isla—The Island Day,*" he says, his smile revealing gold teeth as he hands me the newspaper.

But just as he reaches for the money, his hand freezes in midair. It looks as though the entire newspaper man had suddenly turned into a photograph.

I realize I've accidentally put the whistle down on the saucer with the coins.

"Oh, *perdón*," I say, but before I can take back the whistle, the newspaper man has grabbed hold of it.

He turns it to and fro in front of his face, and then he holds it up close to one eye, as though he were a jeweler and the whistle were a diamond. He looks at it very strangely; I can't tell whether he thinks it's beautiful or ugly, or why he's investigating it so closely in the first place.

He hastily glances around him.

"You know just where the storm came from last night, don't you?" he asks.

I'm too shocked to say anything.

"You know." He gives a nervous nod. "You know about it. *Tú lo sabes.*"

He looks up at the sky.

"There'll be a full moon soon, *sí, sí*," he murmurs. Then he looks back at me. "Are the five hundred full moons over at last? I've stopped counting."

"They'll be over the day after tomorrow," I say. I hesitate slightly before I ask him, "How do you know about Lunalos?"

It's all absolutely bizarre—the sun's burning on the back of my neck, and I'm holding the newspaper in my hand, and my parents are in a shoe store. Lunalos doesn't belong here at all. No, this is our vacation town, and I want a set of bocce balls and maybe a hazelnut ice cream. Or frozen yogurt? Actually, I've started liking frozen yogurt best. I try to slip away secretly in my thoughts so I don't have to think about what a coward I am all over again.

"I made a terrible mess of it back then!" I hear the newspaper man saying.

He fiddles with a scruffy black fingerless glove on his left hand. I've been wondering why he wears a glove in this hot weather.

"Made a mess of what?" I ask.

"Little *señorita!*" He sounds very agitated now, even though he's whispering. "More than forty years ago, I was supposed to free Lunalos, but…"

"Free Lunalos?" I interrupt him in excitement. "You were supposed to free Lunalos?"

"*Sí,* yes, Lunalos, the bathing terrace," the newspaper man says with a nod. He runs his gloved hand across his forehead, where sweat is now glinting. Drips are running down his left temple, unhindered. "But that monster, *este diablo, la…*"

"The vile toad?"

"Yes, that she-devil—I couldn't beat her."

He slumps down in his newspaper stand, and now I can only see the top half of his head. Perhaps he's sat down.

"I didn't look her in the eyes—that toad hates that more than anything."

"So you've really seen her with your own eyes!" I say. "And then, what happened then?" I ask nervously, looking back at the shoe store.

I hope Dad's trying on at least twenty different pairs of sandals as usual so it will take a while until they come out again!

"Then?" The newspaper man cradles his head in his hands. "The vile toad screeched with laughter! She couldn't stop laughing, that she-devil. She was so triumphant about the next five hundred full moons!" He's submerged in his thoughts for a long moment. "All the others were desperately unhappy. Because I'd made a mess of it!" He's very pale in the face now. "And then she gave me something to remember her by," he says at last. "Let me show you something nobody else knows about."

Very slowly, he pulls the glove off his hand. But it's too dim inside the newspaper stand, so at first I can't see the hand he reveals underneath it. He reaches it gingerly out to me, but not without taking a hurried look around first.

And then I see it! I see that the newspaper man has webbed fingers! All the way up to the tips. The skin stretches between his fingers like pale green tracing paper and folds back together as he spreads and closes his fingers.

"That was the devil toad's thanks for my attempt to break her power." The newspaper man gives a bitter laugh. "Do you think anyone would buy my papers if they had to look at this ugly hand?" Hastily, he pulls the glove back on. "I'm not a normal human being like this! And I'm not the only one on the island she's done something like this to!" He leans forward to me. "Take a good look around in the town—there are plenty of people who bear her mark!"

"How old were you back then?" I ask him.

He puts his hand on his chin and looks up.

"*Diez años*—I must have been ten years old," he says at last, more to himself than to me.

Ten years old. Like me, I think. A noisy moped chugs past us. Someone screams something and laughs.

"They want *me* to try it this time," I say quietly.

The newspaper man nods.

"Yes, I can tell by the whistle," he says. He stands up and reaches his human hand across the counter to mine. "I beg you, think carefully about it! She won't spare you either."

He presses my hand firmly. "The devil is in that toad! She harms not only Lunalos, but our whole island with her magic, her storms, *con su alma negra*, with her dark soul!"

He's been getting louder and louder, and now he's out of breath and I can tell he's trying to calm down again.

"What do you think?" I interrupt him. "Why does it have to be a girl who tries to save Lunalos this time when it was a boy last time?"

The newspaper man shrugs his shoulders.

"Oh, you know, it's a very old rule," he says, smiling again at last. "Dark and light, man and woman, *sol y sombra*. There always has to be a balance and justice for something to have a chance to succeed."

Lost in thought, he wipes a little dust from a shelf with his gloved hand. I notice there are still tears trickling down his left cheek; it's almost a waterfall.

"When you're grown up, you have to make sure there's a balance, that everything's fair, *Señorita* Kat. Always remember that! Not many people think of it. Someone always falls by the wayside. Some people always have to work harder for their happiness than others!" He suddenly sounds angry, and he hands me back my money. "You can have the newspaper for free. Read what damage the vile toad has done this time. And be careful, *por favor*! She's really mean and nasty!"

"There's a problem anyway," I say quietly, shooing away a fly. I'm terribly ashamed all over again.

"What kind of a problem?" asks the newspaper man.

"I can't even swim," I say in a rush.

"Oh!" says the newspaper man, and then he's quiet for a moment. "Not at all?"

I shake my head. He strokes his chin in thought.

"That makes the whole thing much more dangerous," he murmurs, so quietly I can barely understand him. "The toad is a perfect swimmer."

My heart's very heavy after all the secrets the newspaper man has told me. Why does it have to be me of all people? There are so many other ten-year-old girls who can at least do the doggy paddle, if not more.

"Can I have my whistle back, please?" I ask. I fold the newspaper and wedge it under my arm.

"Oh yes," mumbles the newspaper man, starting to look around the newspaper stand. "Now where did I put it? I just had it. How strange," he says in the end, looking remorseful. "I can't find it right now, *señorita*. Can you come and get it tomorrow? I'll have found it by then, *seguro*."

"*Señor* newspaper man!" I whisper. "I have to get that whistle back! It's important for…"

I suddenly hear a voice behind me.

"*Buenos días*, everybody, and *arrivederci!*"

It's Dad.

The newspaper man and I look each other firmly in the eyes one more time. Then I take my newspaper and wave with it.

"*Adiós*," I say, smiling.

"See you tomorrow, *señorita*," the newspaper man says quietly.

"*Arrivederci*'s not Spanish, Dad, it's Italian!" I say under my breath as we walk away.

"And 'everybody' is not Italian either, it's English—so what?" he says.

Dad's impossible, really he is.

★5★
Sleeping

I meander along behind Mom and Dad in the orange afternoon sunlight. I'm glad they're strolling so slowly because that gives me enough time to look more closely at the people on the streets and outside the stores.

I soon notice an old woman sitting on a crooked basketwork stool outside a jewelry store. She's wearing a boot on her left foot and a sandal on the right one. Nobody seems to find that surprising; she's an old woman, and when you're old you're allowed to be as strange as you like.

But what if there's something hidden inside that boot that's not a foot? The very moment I pass by her, she stands up and takes a bow. I hear her murmuring, "Kat, noble Kat, *por favor*, help us!" and I get such a shock I hurry away. Mom and Dad haven't noticed anything, thank goodness.

All of a sudden, I hear a kitten meowing! There are so many cute cats on the streets here, and I look around for the one that's screeching so pitifully. A narrow alleyway leads between two stores. I stop and look down the alley. It's very dark down there because the sunlight can't make its way between the closely built houses. Red and white flowers are hanging from the barred windows at the very top. At last, I spot an adorable tabby cat in the semidarkness. I narrow my eyes to slits, hardly making anything out in the dark alley. A young woman in a black dress is standing outside an open door, emptying a bucket of soapy water. The kitten jumps up at her like crazy, screeching and meowing.

The woman whispers, "*Por favor, gato, déjame en paz.* Leave me in peace, cat!"

She wipes one hand on her hip, and then I see for a second, just a tiny moment, a piece of an eel peeking out of her black sleeve. It thrashes about under her dress like a snake! The woman looks around, spots me, looks shocked for a moment, and then disappears into the house, as quick as a flash. The cat tries to slip in behind her, but the door closes in front of its nose.

It's dark in the alley, I try to tell myself. Sometimes you see things in the darkness that aren't real, like eel arms. I stand there motionless, rooted to the spot.

"Kat!" Mom calls over her shoulder, and I jump. "Come on, get a move on!"

At last I can move normally again.

I walk on hastily, faster and faster. In the end I run past two children carrying neon-green styrofoam surfboards, almost stumbling over the metal feet of an ice cooler and totally out of breath by the time I catch up with Mom and Dad.

"Did you see that man just now?" Mom's just asking.

"The fisherman?" asks Dad quietly.

"Yes, him," whispers Mom.

"Why are you whispering?" I whisper.

Mom turns around, and I do the same. A bearded man is standing out front of his store, skillfully slitting open silvery fish stomachs and gutting them. There's something strange about his face.

"I could have sworn he had gills under his beard," whispers Mom as we walk. "It really looked a bit like that, didn't it, Andrew? Really funny!"

A cold shudder runs down my back, under my sweaty T-shirt.

"It looked like that to me," says Dad.

Oh Mom, oh Dad.

There really is something funny going on here, but it's no laughing matter. It's yellow and as large as a soccer ball, and it has a name.

It's the vile toad. But you two don't know a thing about it.

The moon shines white and bright into my room when I creep into bed. The swimming lessons, the thing with the newspaper man, and the hidden enchantments all around me have worn me out. I fall asleep the moment my head hits the pillow.

Or maybe I didn't fall asleep. Maybe I climbed down the rope ladder? Maybe I walked through the deserted town?

All of a sudden, I'm standing on the little path above Lunalos. Everything seems the same as ever: the wind, the quiet, the pine trees. The sea glinting in the moonlight. But when I look over the little wall down to the bathing terrace, I get a terrible shock.

★6★
Waking

There's someone lying on his back on the concrete. He's not moving. But I still know right away that whoever it is is really scared. I quickly squint my eyes to see better. And now, mingled with the warning screech of a gull, I hear the vile toad's mocking laugh. And just after that I see her: yellow and large as a soccer ball.

"You dare to face me again, you loser?" she squeals.

I see her pointing the tip of a wand toward the person lying on the ground before her. Right between his eyes.

"You must be out of your mind!" she squeals again.

The sea, which has been quiet and peaceful up till now, begins making waves, which slap up against the terrace.

Then I hear the prisoner's voice pleading: "Have mercy, *por favor!*" And now I know who it is down there! "Haven't you done enough damage? Haven't you had enough after all your cruelties in the last forty years, toad, *diablo?*"

He seems pretty daring to me, considering what a terrible situation he's in. The toad is still holding her wand between his eyes. Now she shakes with laughter, and the sight of it scares me almost to death—the tip of her wand strokes to and fro between my friend's eyes as she laughs. "Enough damage? *Enough?* Ridiculous! That word doesn't even exist for me, you dirty little weakling!"

She runs the tip of her wand slowly over the newspaper man's nose and chin, then along his neck, finally coming to a halt at his chest.

"I want *everything* or nothing!" she screams. "Neither you nor that girl, that cowardly child with her braids, can stop me from getting what I want!"

The waves have grown larger and louder, and I have to make a real effort to make out the voices over the surf.

"I want power, total and sole power!" she calls.

"But spare the girl, for heaven's sake!" I hear the newspaper man pleading. "Don't put a spell on her like you did to me and all the others!"

The toad is suddenly still. Is she thinking about what the newspaper man said? For a moment, I really believe it—perhaps it's the hope that breaks through hard asphalt like a flower in times of great fear.

"Spare that cowardly thing?" she hisses evilly in the end, throwing her head back and giving a resounding laugh up to the night sky. "I will spare nobody. I'm not in the world to spare anyone! And this time I won't even *have* to spare anyone because that girl doesn't have a grain of courage in her bones. She won't even come tomorrow."

To my horror, she points her wand back between the newspaper man's eyes. I don't dare to make a sound.

"So, you idiot," I hear her droning voice. "I'll give you another souvenir from Lunalos so you won't forget our meeting!"

"Oh no, *por favor, déjame*, leave me be, I beg of you!" implores my friend, and it sounds as though he's hoarse.

But the toad recites:

"You shall never forget your great weakness,
For on it I'll take my revenge—
With magic most painful and cruel!
It gives me strength to live
And to you I shall give
A souvenir to show you're a fool!"

Now she draws invisible signs above the newspaper man's face with her wand. I can see him trembling with fear. I'm frozen with shock.

The toad calls out again.

"One, two, three,
Your face shall be free!"

My friend's face suddenly vanishes. There's nothing to see beneath his hair. Nothing. How can this be? The toad continues.

"Four, five, six,
And seven and eight,
Where is his face?
What is his fate?"

Now she jumps up and down, turns in a circle, and gives a laugh so shrill it hurts my ears.

"Where is his face? What is his fate?
It seems to be lost, but it's not too late.
I'll magic him a new countenance—the perfect piece of evidence!

"Flick—flack—fish,
Hop into your dish!
Anarhichas lupus!"

At that very moment, the toad blocks my view. All I can see is her back hopping up and down, and all I can hear is her screeching and laughing. The newspaper man leaps up, holding his hands in front of his face, and runs off. The vile toad laughs and laughs. My friend will be at the gate any minute now, and I'll be able to see him. Any minute now...

I jump in shock.

The moon's shining bright on my face and on the white bedsheet. Next to me is the wooden closet, and below me I can see the blue star pattern on the stone tiles. I'm in my room, in the guesthouse, and Mom and Dad are sleeping in the next room!

I've been dreaming. I was dreaming.

I rub my hands firmly across my face and take a deep breath, my heart hammering in my chest.

Thank goodness, I think. Thank goodness. It was all just a dream, a terrible nightmare. The vile toad crept into my sleep like ants into a closet.

I'm wide awake now.
The time on my alarm clock is three a.m.
The dream seemed so awfully real, though.
But I'm here, and Lunalos is far away.
What's happened to my friend the newspaper man?
I get out of bed.
I pull on some clothes.
Then I swing my legs onto the windowsill, climb down the rope ladder, and jump onto the gravel path.

★7★

Newspaper Stand

It's much easier to find the way to the newspaper stand than to Lunalos, even at night. All I have to do is walk down the street from the guesthouse, through a little intersection, and then turn left directly onto the promenade. From there, I go straight on for a while past the stores and stalls with their shutters down. I have to walk past the big palm tree and then the two dark blue flowerpots with the bird of paradise flowers. Behind the fountain on the little cobbled square at the end of the promenade is the newspaper stand.

I see it from far off. As I come closer to the little hut, I spot a note fluttering in the wind on the brown wooden shutters, held in place only by a pin. I smooth it out and read it.

"Closed until further notice due to sickness."

How strange. The newspaper man didn't look at all sick yesterday, apart from his webbed hand of course. But he's had that for more than forty years! What's going on here? I knock at the shutters. My knuckles make such a loud noise on the wood that I jump, as though the vile toad had given one of her resounding laughs. A startled rat runs across the square, disappearing behind the fountain. The buzzing of the cicadas falls suddenly silent.

Very quietly, I creep around the newspaper stand. I discover a door at the back, with all sorts of old front pages stuck to it. I lean my face up to the yellowed paper and call quietly, "Newspaper man?"

I jiggle the door handle.

"Are you in there? It's me, Kat!"

At that moment, I feel a hand on my shoulder. I instantly go hot with shock. Someone says, "*Qué pasa, señorita? Estás sola aquí? Dónde están tus padres?*"

Just stay nice and calm. With a smile, I turn around. I see a policeman standing there. He raises one eyebrow and gives me a severe look. Oh no! It's the middle of the night, and I'm a ten-year-old girl, all alone out on the street! And I'm not only all alone—I'm also very bad at telling lies and even worse at Spanish, which makes everything twice as bad. And I didn't understand a single word he just said!

My heart thuds like a machine, and I'm afraid the policeman must be able to hear it. My ears start to glow. I give him a silent smile back and point at the newspaper stand. Time seems to stretch itself out, and I simply creep deep inside myself and wait. I wait and wait.

And at that moment I'm saved.

"*Hija?*" The newspaper man's voice sounds from inside the newspaper stand. "*Estás tú? Venga, adelante!*"

The door opens a tiny crack. I grab the handle and say, "*Gracias, señor, y mucha suerte.*" Thank you, sir, and good luck. What must he be thinking, when a child all on her own wishes him good luck in the middle of the night? "*Tu padre?*" he asks, still slightly suspicious. He nods at the door of the newspaper stand.

"*Si, si.*" I give a cheerful nod, wave, slip in through the door, and close it behind me.

Exhausted by the shock, I lean against the door and listen as the policeman waits outside the newspaper stand for a moment and then walks away at last. His footsteps get quieter and quieter, until I can't hear them anymore. It's pitch black all around me; I can't even see my own hands. There's a smell of wood and old newsprint, a bit like melon.

"What does *hija* mean?" I ask into the darkness.

"Daughter," I hear the newspaper man say.

The voice came from my left, in the corner. I turn in his direction, still not seeing anything.

"What's the matter with you, newspaper man?" I ask. Why on earth is he sitting here in the middle of the night, wide awake in total darkness?

There's a rustling sound, as though he were opening a drawer and rummaging around in it.

"I...I had a bad dream about...about you...and about Lunalos and the vile toad," I stutter, suddenly finding it strange myself that I've come here in the middle of the night. "You were in danger, and the toad did something to your face, something terrible..." I swallow. "But then I woke up before I saw your face."

A fly buzzes close past my ear. In the distance, outside, a dog barks. At last I hear my friend give a deep sigh. In a strange singsong voice, he says, "Your dream was a dream and not a dream at the same time."

All of a sudden I'm scared. It's still absolutely dark, and I can't tell anymore where anything is. I turn a circle on the spot. At least I think I do. Where's the door I just came in by?

"Would you turn the light on, please?" I ask, trying to make my voice sound calm. "I can't see you at all!"

"In a minute you'll wish I'd left the light off," replies the newspaper man.

And I hear a switching sound. The ray of a flashlight slices through the darkness, lighting up his face. I catch my breath.

I'm looking into a monstrous fish face.

Huge fleshy lips, with long yellow teeth protruding between them, open and close slowly. Scaly gray skin wrinkles around them. A hump rises above the lips. To the left and right, dull eyes are stuck behind thick, slimy lids.

"Wha-what is it?" I burst out, feeling for the door handle behind my back. My instinct tells me it's better to get out of here.

The newspaper man suddenly trains the flashlight on my face. Blinded, I lift one arm in front of my eyes.

"Was that *her*?" I ask, noticing I've started to tremble all over. "Was it the vile toad?"

The newspaper man inches toward me.

"Who else could it have been?" he asks.

I've just found the door handle when the newspaper man reaches me, grabbing me by the arm.

"*Perdón, Señorita* Kat," he says. "Your excursion ends here."

He grabs tighter and thrusts me onto a chair. The ray of the flashlight flits around the room like a ghost.

"But what are you going to do to me?" I ask. "I thought we were friends!"

Now he starts tying my arms and legs. He smells of fish. His face is the ugliest thing I've ever seen, worse than the empty space in my dream.

"Friends…" he murmurs, as though he were trying to remember the word, and he knots the rope so tightly around my wrists that it hurts. Then he says out loud, "You're staying here until the full moon is over. Then I can be sure you won't get the stupid idea of freeing Lunalos."

What?! What is he talking about?

"But you must want me to free Lunlalos too!" I call out. "Everyone here wants that! To put a stop to the evil magic at last! Don't you remember?"

For a very brief moment, I see a spark of happiness light up his face as he says, "If I keep you prisoner here, the toad will give me my true face back, and that's not all!" He holds up his gloved hand. "I'll get my hand back too!"

His fishy lips form a cruel smile. He's probably laughing.

The toad has fooled the newspaper man! He's fallen for her tricks, I think desperately.

"And what about all the others under her spells? What about the storms that destroy everything?" I call. "Don't you care about them anymore?" I stare at him in horror. "You said I should always make sure things are fair in this world! What's come over you? What has the toad done to you?"

I almost start crying.

"I'm leaving you alone now," he says, as though he hadn't heard a word I said. He looks at me with his dull eyes, and his voice sounds like a robot. "And so that no one can hear you calling for help, I'm afraid I have to…"

He stuffs a rag in my mouth.

"*Perdón, hija!*" he whispers, switching out the flashlight and disappearing through the back door.

★8★
Owell

There I sit in the dark.

Fear begins to creep up me like cold, damp fog. I push my tongue against the gag. It's so dry! My eyes prick with tears. I have to stay very still and breathe calmly, I think. Stay perfectly still and breathe. Slowly, I breathe in through my nose, and out again just as slowly. In and out.

What will Mom and Dad do when they don't find me in my bed in the morning? They'll call the police and start a search, and they'll be terribly scared. Dad will start crying, and Mom will get huge pupils like she always does when she's upset. I give a cautious jiggle on my chair, moving my legs. It's no use! The newspaper man has done a good job—the ropes are tight. But I absolutely have to get back to my room before dawn!

I think and think for quite a long time. But I just can't come up with any way to get free.

But there! What was that? Didn't I just hear a noise?

I listen as hard as I can, out into the black darkness.

No, everything's silent. I must be mistaken. A fly buzzes past my ear again. That must have been it. Or maybe not!

Now I hear a faint scratching noise. And then a patter of feet.

"Darnation! Oh, watch your language!" comes a sudden high voice in the darkness.

I jump with shock.

"You'd think I had a good nose like all my kind, but no, I run into the table leg like a prize idiot! And don't say that either, oh no, you stop all this darn cursing!"

There's more scratching and pattering, this time very close. Something tickles my ankles and bumps into my skin, slightly damp. It's spooky.

"What on earth is that smell?" the voice whispers.

I hear snuffling.

"It smells like…smells like, good Lord, it's on the tip of my tongue. I know it—we learned it at school. It smells like…"

I give a pathetic whimper through my gag.

"If only I could remember what that smell is!" the voice squeaks excitedly. "I've had just about enough of my useless sniffer, really I have. I've had it up to here!"

There's a sudden silence. The chattering creature takes a short, sharp breath.

"I've got it!" it calls out. "Eureka in the middle of the night! I've remembered what it is! It smells of *human being*."

I whimper as loudly as I can whimper.

"A human being, the female kind. Hmm, let's have a look. But it's too dark to see here; it's accursed and devilish dark in this here shed. Oops, I've gone cursed again. But so what? I don't give a fat rat's tail, I really don't!"

What on earth is this funny creature? I think.

"A human being girl," the creature thinks out loud, and then it falls silent for a while. "Oh hell's bells!" it squeals suddenly. "It must be *the* human being girl! The one and only! How could I not have noticed right away? I'm so dumb, I really am!"

There's an excited pattering to and fro. "Human being girl?" the voice calls up to me.

I whimper in reply.

"I've just remembered something serious! The Water Knight sends his regards and asks whether all is well, for he was concerned that things might be looking bad for you."

The Water Knight has sent me a messenger, I think, excited. Does he know I'm trapped in here? I jiggle my chair and whimper, and the wooden legs creak like crazy.

The creature tut-tuts.

"Oh my goodness, now I realize! The noble human being girl is gagged, and that's why she's so very quiet! How could I not have noticed? How typical, I'm such a *useless* rat!"

A rat! My skin instantly breaks out in goose bumps.

"I'll just hop up there to you, my dear!" she squeaks with a giggle.

I can feel her climbing up the outside of my pant leg. She must be quite large, because her weight pulls at my jeans quite a lot. Her claws scratch me, and I give a muffled wail.

"My apologies, I haven't had a pedicure for a while," she says, and then she gives a hefty sneeze.

I can feel that she's sitting on my lap now. I can't see her, even though she's up so close to me. It's just too dark.

"You must know, noble human being girl Kat," she starts in, working away at the ropes around my hands at the same time. I'm so glad to feel her teeth gnawing close to my wrists. "You must know," she repeats, "that rats are an *intelligent* kind of animal. We're well known for it, oh yes, and *I'm* lucky enough to be one!"

The she falls silent. I hear a steady low noise, like someone secretly nibbling a cookie under the bedcovers. At last I feel something coming loose around my wrists.

"Ha, I'd have bet my speedy rat's fanny that I'd make it in less than two minutes!" She takes one last bite. "And I made it in less than *one* minute. *Voilà*, noble Kat, you're free!" she says in triumph.

I wrench my hands apart and tear the cloth out of my mouth, coughing and gagging. "Thank you!" I force out. "Thank you so much, Rat!"

The rat jumps down from my lap.

"Oh well," she says.

I undo the knots around my ankles.

"No, don't be so modest. You've saved me, and I'm really, really grateful—honest!" I say. At last my feet are free too, and I rub my ankles.

The rat clears her throat.

"No, you misunderstood me," she says. "I was introducing myself, so you don't have to call me *Rat*. We're good friends now, aren't we? My *name* is Owell!"

I get up. I really have no idea what direction to take.

"Owell, do you know where the exit is?" I ask.

Owell seems to find this very amusing.

"Do I know where the exit is, she asks me!" she blurts out. "Goodness me, noble Kat, if you're in trouble, always follow the rats. We old trash-eaters *always* know where the exit is, darn it!"

I wait a moment.

"Don't say that," I scold her.

And then both of us burst out laughing so hard, in the middle of the pitch-dark newspaper stand, without ever having seen each other, that it's a wonderful moment. Owell squeaks and growls and squeals, and I have tears running down my cheeks!

"Aaahh," I sigh, wiping my eyes dry. "Let's get out of here, Owell, OK?"

"Oh yes, darn it!" calls Owell. "Hold onto my back and follow me!"

I bend down, feeling about in the darkness, find her rough fur, and stick to her. I soon bump my head against something hard.

"Ouch!"

"That ouch also happens to be the exit," says Owell.

I'm so glad the door's not locked. The newspaper man must have been in a hurry and thought the ropes would be enough to stop me! Huh!

I open the door, blinking. By the yellowish light on the far-off hills, I can tell dawn is on its way.

★9★
Sneezing

Owell is really rather large with lovely reddish fur. Tiny pink ears peek out of it. And a blue stud glints on one of them.

"How did you manage to bring me a message from the Water Knight without the toad punishing you?" I ask in admiration—I can't spot any kind of enchantment on her.

A gust of wind rustles the palm leaves above us. Owell strokes a paw over her fur, as though she were a movie star in front of a camera.

"Well, now," she says and gives a conceited little cough. "She didn't catch me! I'm obviously in possession of an unmistakable, unique, extremely speedy rat's fanny, if you get my meaning."

I can't help laughing.

"And aside from that," adds Owell with a tug at her glittery blue earring, "this gift from my aunt protects me from evil powers. You know, that aunt really liked me, and she said a child with a name like Owell at least has to be jazzed up with a nice piece of jewelry!"

I'm starting to like Owell.

"Why are you called 'Owell' in the first place, Owell?" I ask, rubbing my poor wrists to get rid of the red marks from the ropes.

She looks down, embarrassed, and sighs.

"Oh, that's simple," she says, her whiskers trembling slightly. "I'm my mother's seventy-seventh and last child, and when I was born she said, 'Oh well, one more doesn't make much difference.' And from then on I've been called after the way she greeted my arrival—Owell. Ha-choo!"

She rubs her nose.

"All the newsprint in that dirty old newspaper stand—yuck, it's no good for me!" She sneezes again. "I'm getting out of here. Off to find a nice stinky trashcan for my breakfast."

And off she patters, dragging her long, pale pink tail behind her.

"Thank you, Owell!" I call after her.

"My pleasure!" she calls back. Then she stops and turns around again. Suddenly she looks very serious. "You take good care of yourself tomorrow night, won't you?"

I don't reply.

Owell turns away, and I hear her murmuring, "Oh, I do hope it turns out all right when she comes up against that nasty dangerous frog at Lunalos. Ha-choo!"

She disappears behind a car tire.

And then something occurs to me.

Quickly, I open the door of the newspaper stand again and go inside. The wooden floor creaks beneath my feet.

The first rays of sun warm my back, lighting everything up now: the closed wooden shutter at the front, all the newspapers on the walls, the chair I was just tied to, and last of all the rope lying gnawed on the ground. And at last a ray of light falls on what I'm looking for: my mother-of-pearl whistle. I put it in my pocket and run back to the guesthouse as fast as I can.

"Good morning, Katinka!"

Mom's yawning in the doorway to my room, stretching her arms to the ceiling and smiling at me. I just climbed into bed and pulled the cover up to my chin about half a second ago.

"You're looking very wide awake!" she says.

That's no surprise, I think.

She comes over to my bed.

"What do you say?" she says. "Shall we try another swimming lesson at our lovely bathing terrace today?"

I go as stiff as a board. No, anything but that! I can't go to Lunalos one day before the full moon! I'd never dare to get in the water today.

"Oh no!" I whine. "But I wanted to—"

"'Oh no' doesn't go," Mom interrupts me with a laugh, tickling me under the cover until I squeak.

Then she stops in surprise.

"Why are you wearing socks?"

I'm really still wearing them. Oh no!

"I was so cold during the night," I say in a rush. And it's not even a lie; I really was cold on my way home.

Mom feels my forehead.

"Aren't you feeling well?" she asks.

"Don't know," I say in a weak voice. "I was sneezing a lot last night."

"Andrew!" Mom gets up. "Andrew, come here a moment—Kat's getting sick!"

Dad comes in my room, sporting boxer shorts printed with elks and a Santa Claus beard made of shaving foam.

"Oh dear, what's up with our champion froggy?" he asks.

"She was sneezing in the night, and she's wearing socks in bed," says Mom, feeling my forehead again. "In this heat!"

I almost feel like I really am sick. Now Dad puts a hand on my forehead. He looks so funny with that white beard and his serious face in the elk boxer shorts. I have to look away so I don't start laughing.

"Rubbish!" he says in the end. "There's nothing wrong with her! A frozen yogurt will soon cool my daughter down, won't it, froggy?"

"And your swimming lesson…" Mom adds.

"Looks like that's a no-no today, a noo-noo, a nee-nee!" Dad sings like an opera singer, dancing back into the bathroom with large skips. We hear him warbling a loud *Don't worry, be happy!* from behind the door.

"Do you think you can still eat ice cream?" asks Mom, concerned.

I give a sigh.

"I guess," I say with a yawn. "But if I could just go back to sleep for a bit first, huh, Mom? I'm so tired from all that sneezing."

"Sure, honey," says Mom with another frown.

Then she leaves me in peace.

"She must have picked something up, I'm sure," I hear her telling Dad.

I turn on my stomach and fall into a deep, deep sleep.

When I finally pad over to Mom and Dad's room, they're lying on the bed looking at a book of photos.

"What are you guys looking at?" I ask, still sleepy.

"Oh, hello there!" calls Dad, turning around. "Our overheated daughter's come back to life. How are we feeling now, huh?"

He grins.

"Let me see if you've got a temperature." Mom waves me over, and I sit down on the bed next to her.

Outside, the sun is burning down on the palm leaves, and a hot wind blows in through the window. I can't help thinking of Owell. I wonder where she is now. I hope she's safe.

Mom's hand is cool on my forehead.

"Hmm," she says, "that feels better, a bit cooler now."

I climb across Mom and crawl into the gap in the mattresses between her and Dad. Then I stare at the page the book is open at, my breath stopping.

"Goodness me, what's up with you now?" asks Mom, looking worried again. "I'll be taking you straight to the doctor if it goes on like this! You're as white as a sheet!" she scolds me.

"What…what's this book?" I finally manage to ask.

"It's an illustrated encyclopedia of fish," Dad explains. "I brought it along from home so I know who I'm dealing with when I go snorkeling. Then I can say a nice polite hello and call my fishy friends down there by their names. Good idea, huh?"

Now all three of us look at the photo on the page.

"Meeting this little guy wouldn't be such fun though," says Dad, tapping the picture.

The photo is the reason I got such a shock. It shows none other than the newspaper man—or rather his terrifying enchanted fishy face! It's so scary, especially now that I've just been sleeping so deeply and had finally forgotten all about Lunalos, the vile toad, and all the rest! And there was nothing I wanted more than to forget it all.

Above the picture is a caption: "Seawolf (*Anarhichas lupus*). Order: Perciformes."

Anarhichas lupus. Isn't that the funny word the vile toad used in her magic spell in my dream? *Anarhichas lupus*. So she changed the newspaper man's face into a seawolf's face! I shudder. That's probably the ugliest fish in the whole book. That toad's just so mean!

"Listen to what they say here." Dad points a finger at the little section of text below the photo of the seawolf.

"The seawolf has a reputation among fishermen as a wild, violent fish that snaps at anything when it is caught. This poor reputation is probably due to its large, wide mouth, from which its powerful teeth emerge." He scratches his head. "Oh no, if I come across this seawolf, I sure won't say hello. I'll make like a fish and flounder out of there!"

He slams the book shut.

"Can you remember that fishy fiend, Kat, so you'll recognize him when you're snorkeling?" he asks.

I nod.

"Oh, I'll remember him," I say quietly. "Don't you worry."

★10★

A Thousand Moons,
a Thousand Shards

At last we're going out for sundaes! The sun's shining, and the sky's pale blue and as high as it gets, so beautiful you want to fly into it. While Mom and I are sitting at a little gray table at the Boléro Café, squabbling over who got the best paper umbrella, Dad disappears.

"Look, you can see the moon already, right here in daylight," says Mom, pointing up at the sky. She bites into a wafer and crunches it up.

"Oh yes," I say, looking up.

And there it is: big and white and full.

"A full moon," murmurs Mom, her mouth full of wafer and frozen yogurt. "You hardly slept during full moons when you were a baby. You used to have bad dreams." She licks her lips. "Let's hope you can sleep tonight, and especially without socks on!"

She smiles at me and dips her long spoon back in her sundae. A little boy is whining at the next table. He wants fries and not "dumb potatoes." And he wants Coke and not orange juice. And he wants...

"Is yours good?" asks Mom.

I put my spoon aside and lean back against my chair. I'm supposed to sleep well. And I'm supposed to eat well too. How on earth can I sit here eating a sundae and thinking about whether I'll sleep well tonight, on the five hundredth *full moon night*, or whether the dumb frozen yogurt's good? How can I?

"Oh no, it's a *thousand* moons!" I whisper, suddenly horrified.

I've just realized that if the newspaper man failed to free Lunalos five hundred full moons ago, there must have been five hundred full moons of imprisonment before that! So the vile toad has been in power for over eighty years—how absolutely awful!

"What do you mean?" Mom looks confused. "Can I have an espresso, please!" she calls out to the waitress, who nods and smiles.

"What? Oh, nothing," I say hastily. "It's just a song by a band, you know?"

"Is it?" says Mom, surprised. "The song's called 'Oh No, It's a Thousand Moons'?"

"That's it, yes," I say.

"That's a nice title. Kind of poetic," says Mom, scraping the bottom of her sundae glass with a clink of her spoon.

I haven't even touched my sundae. I'm suddenly feeling so silly in this vacation resort, surrounded by stupid screaming children who just want to get something bought for them and don't even notice what's going on here on the island. Even the sky's not as blue as it's supposed to be on vacation, I think. Thick clouds have suddenly started gathering.

And then Dad comes back, swinging a little case of bocce balls in one hand with a grin.

"Hey, princess," he says with a wink. "How about a new handbag?"

Oh, Dad.

But I pull myself together.

I say a loud "Oh wow!" but it doesn't sound convincing because all of a sudden I don't want to be this Kat anymore, the Kat with her head full of frozen yogurt and bocce balls instead of a heart full of courage. I'd much rather be the noble Kat, the savior of Lunalos!

"Ouch!"

Mom suddenly grabs her arm, making a face.

"Ow!" says Dad too, and he holds the bocce case up over his head.

I look up at the sky—it's pitch black now! And there! Something hard and ice-cold hits me right below one eye. A huge hailstone! As quick as a flash, I jump up and my chair falls to the ground with a crash. The people all around us are starting to scream and run away. The boy at the next table is still yelling, "Fries! I want *fries!*"—holding his hands over his head and crying. At that moment, a mighty bolt of lightning flashes across the black sky. "Run, son!" his mother shrieks, dragging him away by the arm. More people are screaming. Some tear open car doors, leap inside, and slam them shut behind them.

"Come on, inside the Boléro, quick!" I call out to Mom and Dad, and we zigzag around the little marble tables and chairs. Dad knocks a sundae glass off one of the tables, and it shatters into a thousand shards with a sound like a high-pitched bell.

Our teeth chattering with the icy cold, we're finally in the shelter of the café. The waitress who just served us frozen yogurt doesn't even look at us. She's gripping her tray to her stomach, looking outside as though hypnotized.

Hail and rain lash across the tables and chairs. The wind knocks over three large flowerpots, and they roll around between the chairs along with more and more huge hailstones. A palm tree gradually leans to one side, and its ceramic pot breaks with a sad crack.

"My goodness, this isn't normal!" Mom whispers, appalled. "A minute ago the sky was bright blue and the sun was burning down like fire, wasn't it, Kat?" She quickly puts an arm around my shoulders.

A thousand moons, a thousand shards, I think. A thousand moons, a thousand shards.

"Yes," I answer quietly, "it was like that just a minute ago."

The waitress turns around slowly and drags her heels to behind the counter. She puts her tray down and lights a cigarette. Blowing the smoke out, she murmurs, "When will this haunting end? When?" Then she hides her head in her hands and gives a sob.

Dad says, "Well, this is an adventure, isn't it, froggy?"

Then he looks over at me and goes pale as a sheet, gasping for air and grabbing at a chair, which he collapses onto like a wet sack.

"What's the matter, Dad?" I ask.

"You've got blood on your face," he says, looking away and holding out a paper tissue. "I can't stand the sight of blood, froggy. Wipe it off, will you?"

I wipe my cheek. That mean hailstone really did injure me below my eye!

"This vacation's turning out to be dangerous!" says Mom, taking the paper tissue out of my hand, licking it, and then dabbing away with it under my eye.

I can't stand it when Mom uses her spit to clean wounds; it makes it really hurt in the first place.

We all sit at a table for a while in silence, waiting. Suddenly the rain lets off.

"It's really not normal—just look at that!" says Dad, getting up and going outside onto the terrace. "Sunshine and steel-blue skies all over again!"

We join Dad outside. He's right. The sky's blue, not a single trace of cloud to be seen. I squint; the sun's shining bright on my eyes. Mom puts on her sunglasses. All the hocus-pocus lasted less than ten minutes. Dad bends over and picks something up.

"Have you ever seen hailstones like this, Eva?" he asks, holding out a sharp-edged ball of ice the size of a fist to Mom.

Mom shakes her head, dumbfounded. I take the stone from Dad's hand. It looks like an uncut diamond. It's ice-cold in my hands, starting to melt instantly. I hold it close up to my eyes. Inside, I see something round and yellow. Or am I seeing things? Isn't that the vile toad? Then there's a voice like a hiss. "Just a reminder: I'm going to win the battle, braid-head!" And then someone laughs.

"What's so funny?" Mom asks me.

I drop the hailstone, and it shatters like glass into a thousand splintered shards.

The vile toad will wreak her cruel havoc for another forty years. Just because I, Kat, am too much of a coward to swim underwater!

I have to try and beat the vile toad and free Lunalos. I just have to.

I suddenly know that, right here outside Café Boléro. I know it for certain.

Mom and Dad have been asleep for ages, and I'm still standing at the window, staring out at the moon. It's as round as a ball, not a single sliver missing. A few scanty clouds drift past it. I look at the whistle shimmering in the moonlight on the windowsill. Somewhere, a dog howls.

And then I go to the closet and get dressed very quietly. Once I have everything on, I realize I'll need my bathing suit! Where is it? I rummage around in my T-shirts, sweaters, and pants until they're all a brightly colored tangle of fabric. Not a bathing suit to be found. It must be in Mom and Dad's bathroom. They probably rinsed out the saltwater and hung it up to dry.

As quiet as a cat, I creep along the guesthouse hallway, where the light is still on, and open the door to their room. The moon is shining brightly on their bed. Dad's head is resting on Mom's shoulder. The door to the bathroom is opposite the room door, and I summon up all my courage.

Like a ghost, I float over the stone floor to the bathroom door. My heart thuds. The door's not closed properly, and I nudge it open, slip inside, and lean against it until it closes behind me. I look for the light switch in the pitch darkness. My fingers feel across cold, smooth tiles, then across the wood of the doorframe, soft, fluffy fabric, and then—there's a crash!

My heart stands still for a few seconds, and then it starts beating again. I must have knocked over a bottle of something; broken glass crunches under my shoes. I hear Dad murmuring something and turning over in bed. I don't dare to move another inch. But neither of them wakes up. Phew! I think; I can't think anything else except "Phew!"

At last I find the light switch and press it. Like a miracle, my eyes instantly alight on my bathing suit on a hanger next to the sink. Quickly, I grab it, turn out the light, and flit out of the bathroom.

"Kat?" I jump. "What are you doing here?" Mom sits up in bed, still half asleep. Dad mumbles something and turns over.

"I, ummm…"

What on earth can I say? My ears feel like they're on fire. I hastily crumple up the bathing suit in my fist behind my back. "I couldn't sleep. It must be because…because of the full moon."

It's not even a lie! No, it's the absolute truth!

Mom gets up and comes over to me. Her hair's mussed up.

"But you're dressed!" she says in surprise.

"I thought I'd go for a walk around the block," I say, "to tire me out, you know?"

Has anyone ever heard a ten-year-old girl say anything that stupid? Not me anyway.

Mom doesn't think much of the idea either.

"Kat, you're kidding!" she says quietly but upset. She steers me out of the door, along the hallway, and back into my room. She switches on the light, and I squint, blinded.

"You get undressed right now, and get back into bed!" She tugs my shirt over my head. "A walk around the block! I never want to hear anything like that from you again, not until you're eighteen years old!"

Then she stops in her tracks, staring at me.

"Why are you holding your bathing suit?"

I'm starting to run out of excuses, but luckily Mom seems to be far too tired to wait for an answer.

"I'm glad you like it so much, but now please take your clothes off!"

She takes the bathing suit firmly away from me and puts it neatly on the chair by my dressing table. I get undressed. Mom holds up my cover, and there's nothing I can do but to get back under it.

"You stay right here. Is that clear?" she asks in a strict voice.

"Crystal clear," I say. "It's just so light, you know?"

"Then close your eyes, for goodness' sake!" she scolds me, rolling her eyes. "I wish I knew what's gotten into you on this vacation, really I do. And now sleep well."

She closes the door behind her.

I've got no time to lose now!

Even more quietly and quickly than before, I put all my clothes back on, with my bathing suit underneath. I put the whistle in my sunglasses case and hang the whole thing around my neck. Then I swing myself out of the window.

★11★
Jumping

This time, I find my way along the streets and alleys as easily as on my way to school. I don't see anyone. When I come to the narrow pathway and see the barred gate, I stop. I'm completely out of breath; I've run almost all the way. I peer over the wall. The sea behind it is as smooth and silver as a mirror. I hesitate. Perhaps it was all a dream after all? It all looks so peaceful.

And then along comes a gust of wind and blows in my face, as though it wanted to wake me up from a nap I shouldn't be taking. It whistles past my ears and lies back down on the still air. At that moment, the gate flies open and swings against the wall with a clang, just like the first day, except that this time nobody's touched the rusty handle. I summon up all my courage and walk through it.

Slowly, one step at a time, I climb down the stairs. It's not until I'm at the bottom that I see the newspaper man standing on the terrace, looking at me with his awful fishy face. Water is dribbling down his left-hand side, dripping into a puddle on the concrete. Before I can think a clear thought, he comes a few steps toward me.

"Don't do it, *Señorita* Kat! I beg you, please don't go to her, please!"

He sounds at his wits' end.

"Don't dive down to her!" he says again.

And now he actually goes down on his knees and lowers his head. The fish scales on top of it glint wet and green in the moonlight.

"She'll put a spell on you like she did to me!" he calls out, looking at me again. He reaches his arms out for me, and now I see that both his hands are webbed! All the way up to his fingertips!

"Forgive me, Kat, *por favor,* I never wanted to harm you. I…was under…her…spell. No one can beat her! You can't either!"

I walk past him very slowly, stopping at the edge of the terrace and looking out across the sea. It looks huge, dark and bottomless.

No! Enough of this! I've had enough of this stupid fear!

Quickly, I strip off my clothes down to my bathing suit. My fingers trembling, I open the sunglasses case, take out the whistle, and blow into it as hard as I can. As usual, I don't hear a sound, but I know that doesn't mean anything. Out of the corner of my eye, I spot the newspaper man coming toward me. I give a hard swallow.

At that very moment, the Water Knight emerges from the water. He pushes a tube toward me with his nose, which I immediately put in my mouth like I did with the snorkel. The other end goes up to the sky. I look up. Above our heads, two herring gulls flutter in the sky, holding the tube in their beaks. They give warning calls.

My head whizzes around. The newspaper man is stretching his fishy hands out for me.

"Don't do it!" he moans.

"Jump!" calls the Water Knight.

And I jump.

At last.

The water closes up over my head, swallowing me whole. I force my eyes open. The saltwater stings. I spot the Water Knight right in front of me.

I have to swim now! I just have to!

What did I learn?

Push the water aside with your hands and arms, and move your legs like a frog. Frog kicks! It all shoots into my mind in a split second. I move my arms and legs with all my might, not giving up. I fight like crazy! I want to move through the water! I want to win against the water! But no matter how hard I try, I hardly get anywhere. It's as though I were crawling through heavy, sticky earth. The Water Knight swims ahead. Desperately, I see him getting smaller and smaller.

I knew it all along. I can't do it. I just can't swim.

"Kat," I hear a quiet but urgent voice say from nearby. "Ka-at." It sounds like a murmur, a rustle, like something that's been there such a long time that you've forgotten to hear it at all.

Haven't I heard that before somewhere?

And all of a sudden, I realize something.

I don't have to fight against the water at all. No. The water and I are as one. I'm the water and the water is me.

It's very simple. I move my arms and legs again, this time only slightly, and I forget everything I've learned. Suddenly, it works! It's so easy! I'm swimming!

I'm swimming.

I'M SWIMMING.

I dive down quickly.

I dive all the way down to the cave.

And there I see the Water Knight, right outside the opening to the cavern. His eyes are closed, and he looks as though he's floating. Blood seeps out of a wound in his side, rising through the water like a thin, pale red cloth.

★12★
Pots

"Water Knight!" I whisper desperately, stroking his flank. "Dear, dear Water Knight, what's happened?"

"I...I don't know. I...save yourself, Kat. I...can't...go on," he says weakly.

And then I'm so mad at that vile toad!

"Don't give up," I say. "I'll be right back!"

On my way to the cave I turn around to hear the Water Knight whispering, "You can swim...like a fish."

The entrance to the cave is a large, almost round opening. I swim through it without scraping anything. And a moment later, I'm in the cave.

There's a strange light in here. It looks warm, as though there were lots of candles or a fireplace burning in the water. I look around. No toad.

The cave is as large as my room at the guesthouse. On one wall, I spot shelves reaching up to the ceiling. I can't tell from here what's on them. I take another look around, expecting the toad any minute now. But there's no toad to be seen anywhere. So I swim right across the room to take a closer look at the collection on the shelves.

What is it the she-devil keeps here?

All along the shelves are neat rows of brown ceramic pots with lids on them. Almost like in my grandma's basement, where she stores her preserves and pickles. But what does the vile toad brew up here? Seaweed jelly? I tug at a lid, and then another, but they stay put on top of the pots. Then I notice little labels stuck to the pots. Each of them says something different, in newspaper-style print.

"Fernando," I read. "Gloria."

I swim slowly to the right.

"Agostin. Karla. Anja."

All different people's names. I swim one shelf up.

"Elisa. Gustavo. Kat."

I almost choke on my breathing tube.

Kat?

Kat?

I swim up so close to the pot that I almost bump my nose on it. No, there's no doubt about it. I read it again: "Kat." The only difference from the other pots is that this one doesn't have a lid on it. I look inside. It's definitely empty.

But why does it have my name on it? And why are all the other people's names on the pots?

"*Cómo estás, Señorita* Kat?"

The voice summons me up from my thoughts.

With a shock, I turn around. My hair, floating around me in slow motion, blocks my view for a second. But really only for a moment.

And then I see him.

"Newspaper man!" I call out.

He laughs. But it doesn't sound at all friendly.

"Yes, yes, it's me, the newspaper man. The newspaper man!" he says with a mocking laugh. Although he still has a human body and legs, he's looking more and more like a fish. "But if I was only the newspaper man, everything would be fine!"

He stares at me.

"Where's the vile toad?" I ask, looking around the cave again.

The newspaper man laughs again.

"The vile toad! Ah, yes. How good that everyone at Lunalos believes in her! There's nothing more useful than a stupid fairy story."

My thoughts start circling like a carousel. The toad—a fairy story?

"But I saw her," I say carefully.

"*What* did you see?" asks the newspaper man, amused.

Suddenly, as he moves for a second, I spot a fin on his back. I didn't see that on the bathing terrace! What can it mean?

"I saw a huge yellow toad. The vile toad," I answer.

The newspaper man falls silent for a moment. Then he says, "That's right, you saw a big yellow toad. But who says that was the vile toad, *hija*? Who has ever seen her doing anything bad?"

He laughs again.

"But the storms!" I interject. I can't believe there is no vile toad.

"Storms have existed as long as the earth has, my little daughter. And there are more and more of them now because you humans treat the world with such disrespect! There are all kinds of terrible storms—without a single stupid vile toad!" He shakes with laughter, the fin on his back trembling along. "People are so simple!"

He suddenly notices me staring at his fin.

"Are you surprised?" he asks, stretching his back slightly in my direction.

"Why are you changing more and more?" I ask.

The newspaper man, who isn't a newspaper man anymore—more like some kind of waterman—says, "The stronger you got, *Señorita* Kat, the weaker I became, and more and more of my human shell fell off. Even when you first came to Lunalos, I woke up the next morning with webbed fingers on one hand!" He gives a bitter laugh. "That's how I knew you might be dangerous for me! But I thought you were a coward and you'd stay that way. I'd never have thought you'd learn to swim so quickly and have the courage to come here at full moon!"

He looks at me, almost admiringly. No, he's looking at me greedily, as though he wanted to swallow me up! *I have to distract him,* I think.

My eyes fall onto the brown pots on the shelf against the wall beside me. I point up to them.

"What do you collect in here?" I ask quickly.

Now the newspaper man is heading my way. Like in a well-practiced water ballet, I swim away from the shelves at the same time, to the other side of the cave. I take a nervous glance at the exit, now far away.

The newspaper man runs his webbed hand along the lids, like Dad with his beloved record collection.

"This is where I collect the powers I need," he says. And as I look puzzled, he adds, "Human powers." He spreads his webbed fingers and looks at them as though they were strange creatures. "I collect the best of them—for example, cleverness and shiny hair and a sense of humor and lovely arms and legs and courage—until I've finally got enough of them all, enough to be a complete human being myself. I don't want to be half and half anymore, a creature between land and sea like I am now! It's such hard work, so terrible. Do you understand, *hija*?"

I don't answer, and he continues.

"I take a little piece of every human who comes close to me. At that moment, they lose power and I keep that power tightly in one of these wonderful clay pots, where it can't escape. The lids are as tight as a drum!" He gestures at the shelves like a conductor toward his orchestra. "They're magnificent powers in my collecting pots! Only from the best, the cleverest, most beautiful people. Take my word for it! When I combine them all within me one day, I'll be an amazing human being, an almost perfect—" He interrupts himself. "No. I'll be *the perfect human being!*"

The newspaper man goes on talking. He talks and talks, not even noticing me carefully opening my sunglasses case, which I'm still wearing around my neck. I take out the whistle and quickly hide it in my clenched fist. Suddenly, something glints between the pots on the shelf. It's something blue. It's—yes, it's Owell's earring! The protective gift from her aunt!

"What have you…what have you done to Owell?" I shout in shock.

The newspaper man instantly stops going on about his "perfect human being" and stares at me. His fishy mouth opens wide, and I see his teeth flashing like rows of soldiers. "Your little rescue rat? I changed her into a maggot," he hisses. "No one goes against me unpunished! And *you* won't either, by the way! Your time's up now—you've developed wonderful powers of courage that I need for myself!"

And then everything happens at the same time. The newspaper man darts toward me like a snake. I take a deep breath through my breathing tube, wrench it out of my mouth, and blow the whistle with all my might. At the same time, I look the newspaper man firmly in the eye, not flinching for a bat of an eyelid from his gaze.

He stops mid-lunge. There's an incredibly loud crunching sound. His ugly head turns toward the shelves. I'm still blowing the whistle, a single long breath with all my strength.

And then something very strange happens: the pots on the shelves start bursting. One after another, like soap bubbles. Their shards give off a dull tinkling sound, sailing slowly through the water like feathers floating on air.

I'm running out of air. Quickly, I take the whistle out of my mouth and put the tube between my lips again. I take a deep breath.

Swimming above the shards now covering the floor of the cave like brown earth is a fish. A rather ugly fish. A fish I recognize from Dad's encyclopedia and my nightmare: *Anarhichas lupus*, the seawolf. It looks at me the way fish look. Pretty fishy. Expressionless. But then I get the feeling it's staring at my breathing tube, and it swims in my direction.

"Don't you dare!" I say threateningly, making a movement as though I wanted to blow the whistle again. And the seawolf darts straight out of the cave.

Something flashes blue in the midst of the pile of shards of shattered pots. As if by magic, Owell's glittery earring hasn't sunk into the sandy ground; it's balancing on a shard! I pick it up and put it carefully into my sunglasses case. Then I swim through the cave exit, back out to the open sea.

I look around in all directions. The Water Knight! He was here a moment ago!

A dolphin swims toward me, as fast as an arrow, with enormous strength. Millions of tiny bubbles fizz around his body like mother-of-pearl beads.

"Noble Kat!" says the dolphin, stopping in the water directly in front of me. His body emits a beautiful glow.

Is this dolphin…? It's impossible!

"When my wound suddenly closed up," he says, and now I recognize the Water Knight's voice, "I knew you'd won your battle!"

He turns an amazing somersault!

"Let us swim to the surface, noble Kat," he says. "I'm getting bored down here!"

Yes, he says it as easy as that, "Let us swim!" And I don't think for a single moment that I can't swim. Because I can! I can swim. Crybaby Kat, who barely dared to put a toe in the water back home, is swimming just as well as a dolphin now!

"Darn it. Where did I leave my earring, that darn blue glittery thing?" squeaks a voice as we surface from the water.

It's none other than Owell.

She's leaping to and fro on the terrace, and she's not a maggot at all—she's a rat just like she always has been. I've never been so pleased to see a rat in my life! I climb up the ladder out of the water and run to her.

"Owell, is everything OK?" I ask breathlessly.

"Oh, what an honor, noble Kat!"

Owell stands on her hind legs and takes a bow.

I'm so incredibly happy to see her again!

"Everything's A-O-ratty-K, oh yes. I'm feeling truly scrumptious!" she says with a wiggle of her backside. "You know my darn speedy rat's fanny is unbeatable! The only thing is, I've lost my aunt's earring—it's enough to drive a girl mad, darn it!"

Owell runs to and fro, sniffing.

"Watch your language!" I scold her, and then I kneel down, open my sunglasses case, and hold the earring in front of my friend's nose. We both spend the next ten minutes laughing like crazy.

★13★

Adiós, Lunalos!

"That fisherman, do you remember?" says Mom to Dad over breakfast. "He didn't have gills under his beard at all. I took another good look yesterday."

"He probably had bad acne as a teenager, and what you saw was the scars," says Dad. "Clear as muddy-dud-mud."

I shove half a bread roll in my mouth at once to stop myself grinning like a Cheshire cat.

And the woman outside the jewelry store's not wearing boots anymore—just sandals on both feet. When I pass her store after the night of the full moon, she stops me, disappears inside, and then emerges to present me with a beautiful velvet box. In it is a ring with a red coral stone. We laugh and bow to each other. Neither of us says a word. We both know what happened, and there's nothing more to say.

Luckily, we still have a few days left on the island. Night after night, I climb down the rope ladder and run all the way to Lunalos. The Water Knight's dolphin leaps now look like pure, glittering joy! He gives me lessons to improve my swimming—he really is a champion swimmer. And I get better and better too!

My last night arrives, and everyone gathers together to say goodbye. They're all there: the Water Knight, the Frisbee fish, Owell, and the two herring gulls.

I take the staircase down to Lunalos for the last time. The wind lifts up my braids like two scraps of paper and lays them gently back down on my shoulders. I turn around. Owell is standing on the terrace, right where I lay on my towel that first day. The Water Knight looks up at me from the sea. I wave.

"*Adiós*, noble Kat!" they all call with a laugh.

"*Adiós*, Lunalos!" I reply.

I open the gate.

Then it's as though I've forgotten something, and I turn around once again.

On the steps behind me perches a fat yellow toad. She looks at me out of green eyes, but not particularly evilly.

"*Adiós*, toad," I whisper.

She doesn't answer, just croaking quietly. I close the gate gently behind me.

We fly home the next morning.

Mom and Dad tell everyone proudly how they taught me to swim. And Ms. Eckhart calls us at home a week after the end of summer vacation and tells Dad she's "astounded" because now I can do a perfect dive and swim faster and more elegantly than anyone else in my class. Almost like a fish, she says.

I don't comment. Nobody would believe me anyway if I told them about Lunalos.

But I know what happened.

And that's good enough for me.

Spanish Glossary

adiós	goodbye
buenos días	good day
Cómo estás?	How are you?
con su alma negra	with his/her black soul
Déjame!	Leave me alone!
diez años	ten years
Dónde están tus padres?	Where are your parents?
Estás sola aquí?	Are you alone here?
Estás tú?	Is that you?
este diablo	that devil
Gato, déjame en paz!	Leave me in peace, cat!
gracias	thank you
hija	daughter
Hola, señorita.	Hello, miss.
Mucha suerte!	Good luck!
padre	father
perdón	excuse me
por favor	please
Qué pasa?	What's up?
seguro	safe, sure
sí	yes
sol y sombra	sun and shade
Tú lo sabes.	You know it.
Venga, adelante!	Come in!

About the Author

Rusalka Reh, born in Melbourne, Australia, in 1970, grew up in Germany. She studied remedial education and art therapy and worked in children's homes. She has been a freelance writer since the year 2000, regularly publishing poetry and prose in magazines and anthologies.

About the Translator

Katy Derbyshire is a translator living in Berlin. She reviews books on the blog "Love German Books."